T0374115

Something Curious
Book 1: Poetry

For children and the wisely curious

Linda P. Jacob

Copyright © 2016 by Linda P. Jacob. 746417

ISBN: Softcover   978-1-5245-3823-1
        Hardcover   978-1-5245-3824-8
        EBook   978-1-5245-3822-4

All rights reserved. No part of this book may
be reproduced or transmitted in any form or by
any means, electronic or mechanical, including
photocopying, recording, or by any information
storage and retrieval system, without permission
in writing from the copyright owner.

This is a work of fiction. Names, characters,
places and incidents either are the product of the
author's imagination or are used fictitiously, and
any resemblance to any actual persons, living or
dead, events, or locales is entirely coincidental.

Print information available on the last page.

Rev. date: 09/08/2016

To order additional copies of this book, contact:
Xlibris
1-888-795-4274
www.Xlibris.com
Orders@Xlibris.com

DEDICATION

Something Curious, Book 1: Poetry
is lovingly dedicated to my grandson,
Eliott – a blessing, a delight and an inspiration.

I also thank the artist of the painting used for the front and back cover of this book: Eliott, who created the artwork just before his 7th birthday in July 2016. He titled his painting, The City.

Acknowledgement

- My children, John Stanley and Joy, for their loving encouragement, advice and wisdom.

Something Curious

Book I: Poetry

Synopsis:

Children astonish us with eager wonderment about the simple mysteries around us – the drop of rain, the stir of the wind, the fall of a lemon, the tease of a tickle, the crackle of a popcorn, or the moo of a cow. Children are awed and their imagination takes flight in trying to understand the routines of the universe in their systemic and pure order.

This book is a celebration of a child's curiosity and love for asking or wondering why. Adults have a lot to learn from a child, not really to challenge the way things are, but to appreciate the complex design that holds all things together, each with its own role and function in the master plan.

Something Curious Book I is written for children and parents who love to read to their children. It also invites the mature and wisely curious to enjoy, even for a moment, in assuming the mind of a child that engages in the why's of the world's simple mysteries.

Waiting for a Lemon

Waiting for a Lemon

I sit under the lemon tree
To watch the ripe lemon fall
I count to a hundred and three
I whistle and coo and call
Yet no ripe lemon falls

I wait under the lemon tree
For something yellow to fall
Alas, no movement from above
I squint my eyes, stare hard and try
To stay awake and gaze up high

Feeling tired my eyelids close
To sleep under the lemon tree
Until light thuds startle me
Two ripe lemons fall on my nose
To wake me from my restful doze

The Tickle

The Tickle

A tickle makes you cringe
A tickle makes you smile
A tickle makes you laugh
'Til you crumble onto a pile

Stop stop that naughty tickle
Can't control continuous chuckle
Sides are bursting, voice is choking
Please please no more joking

Now no one's tickling, no one's teasing
My jovial giggles just keep bursting
Can't stop imagining that funny tickle
More please, oh I'm hopelessly fickle

The Popcorn

The Popcorn

I hear things crackle and pop
In a bag, they stir and don't stop
Daddy put in something flat
The bag has grown big and fat

Soon all the crackling stops
Daddy, careful the bag is hot
Hold it so no popcorn drops
Let's eat, there's really a lot

I see a popcorn roll on the floor
Get it before the ten-second rule
Into my mouth that saved one goes
And more 'cause I'm not yet full

Oh no the bag is nearly empty
Some at bottom stayed unpopped
When all the crackling stopped
Cooked popcorn fluffed on top

A Staring Squirrel

A Staring Squirrel

There's that curious little gray squirrel
Perched on a branch of the acacia tree
Staring at me wide eyed and mischief free
Ready to hop at the whistling wind's sway
Or the tweaking twig that stands on its way

I stare back at the wide-eyed squirrel
That ogles and asks for no lively quarrel
It doesn't smile but wears a pleasant look
Wants to befriend me, so I'll read it a book
About a gray squirrel on a tree's shadowy nook

Old Brown Sneakers

Old Brown Sneakers

Anyone seen my old brown sneakers
Mommy threw them 'cause they squeak
I wanted to keep them so I bawled
Cried hard 'til I could hardly speak

Please find my old brown sneakers
No mind if they squeak and squeak
Comfortable on my tiny feet
When I walk on the muddy street

Squeak squeeze squeak squeeze
As I splash on the muddy street
I run around as I sneeze and sneeze
My old brown sneakers on my feet

My old brown sneakers I finally see
Under my wooden bed sitting free
Happily I put them on so fast
But oh my feet had grown a blast

The Wind

The Wind

Something tugs at my hair
And brushes my cheeks
Is it the wind
Yet I do not see the wind

Something speaks to me
In a loud hush and a whir
Is it the wind
Yet I do not see the wind

Something blows my satin skirt
To make that swooshing noise
Is it the wind
Yet I do not see the wind

Something plays with the trees
That sways its branches and leaves
Is it the wind
Yet I do not see the wind

Something blows the ocean waves
To rise and fall in cascades of lace
Is it the wind
Yet I do not see the wind

Something halts me as I walk
Pushes me back to whence I came
Is it the wind
Yet I do not see the wind

I know the wind is there
I know it's there
I do not see it
But I know it's there

Call of the Rain

Call of the Rain

I hear the pitter-patter of rain

It knocks on my window pane

I do not want it to come in

Why would it want to come in

I hear the splashing of rain

Loudly against my window pane

I do not want it to come in

Why would I want it to come in

I watch the pushy falling rain

It beckons come and prance about

Why would I want to dash out

That would be so insane

I reach out to catch the dropping rain

It pours gently now on the lane

I think I want to come out and play

That surely would brighten my day

Thunder and Lightning in a Storm

Thunder and Lightning in a Storm

Have you heard thunder roar
Its voice is like a lion's growl
The sound can surely roll
Like animals in a nasty brawl

Have you seen lightning flash
So sudden in a bold rush
Its light shines bright with glare
Its glitter is just an ugly snare

Thunder, lightning, whooping wind
Then pounds the thud of heavy rain
Close your eyes and plug your ears
Just sleep and dream away your fears

The Master's Order

The Master's Order

Why do doggies bark and kitties purr

Can't doggies purr and kitties bark

Why do roosters crow and cattle moo

Can't roosters moo and cattle crow

Why do horses neigh and frogs croak

Can't horses croak and frogs neigh

Why do bees buzz and birds chirp

Can't bees chirp and birds buzz

Why does rain fall and cloud float

Can't rain float and cloud fall

Why does morning dawn and twilight dusk

Can't morning dusk and twilight dawn

All creatures and all creation

Follow paths in their formation

No diverging no exchanging

Proper roles and no confusing

Master Master does it matter

If we wonder and often ponder

How each created is so mandated

With perfect order coordinated

Thanks to One Who's Here and There

Thanks to One Who's Here and There

Thank you for today

It really came out nice

Everything good I say

Even had ice cream thrice

Protected Mommy and Daddy

Lil' sister and me completely

Closely watched over our toys

Left outside for neighboring boys

I pray for fun again tomorrow

For all tomorrows that come and go

And friends who come to play

And eat our cookies later in the day

You live up there with stars afar

Yet you're down with all of us here

How can that be, you're here and there

You're always near, and love us so dear

Linda P. Jacob

Linda P. Jacob's writing experience over the years includes features on culture in international magazines, news and religion stories, theater and music reviews for the local paper.

She has embarked on projects designed around literary expression in poetry and prose. She recently started working on expression in music and lyrics, a lively interest that sparks her creative endeavors.

A California resident, she worked in administrative, management and finance jobs at a local daily newspaper and university.

Now a zesty grandmother, Linda finds inspiration for her works in her family and her faith.

Printed in the United States
By Bookmasters